Night of the Veggie Monster

GEORGE McCLEMENTS

BLOOMSBURY
CHILDREN'S
BOOKS

Copyright © 2008 by George McClements

Typeset in Billy
Art created with mixed media
Book design by Amy Manzo Toth

Published by Bloomsbury U.S.A. Children's Books
175 Fifth Avenue, New York, NY 10010
Distributed to the trade by Holtzbrinck Publishers

Library of Congress Cataloging-in-Publication Data
McClements, George.
Night of the Veggie Monster / by George McClements. — 1st U.S. ed.
p.   cm.
Summary: Every Tuesday night, while his parents try to enjoy their dinner,
a boy turns into a monster the moment a pea touches his lips.
ISBN-13: 978-1-59990-061-2 • ISBN-10: 1-59990-061-0 (hardcover)
ISBN-13: 978-1-59990-234-0 • ISBN-10: 1-59990-234-6 (reinforced)
[1. Food habits—Fiction. 2. Vegetables—Fiction. 3. Behavior—Fiction.
4. Family life—Fiction. 5. Humorous stories.] I. Title.
PZ7.M1325Nig 2008   [E]—dc22   2007017850

First U.S. Edition 2008
Printed in China
(hardcover) 10 9 8 7 6 5 4 3 2 1
(reinforced) 10 9 8 7 6 5 4 3 2 1

37651246   7/08

Green Is Good

Finicky Eaters

Vegetables 4 Kids

For my
sweet peas:

Rachel, Samuel,
and Matthew

Something **TERRIBLE**
happens every Tuesday night.

It's not the **pork chops** or the **mashed potatoes**. It all starts when I'm forced to eat . . .

Time for another fun-filled hour.

They have no idea what

does to me.

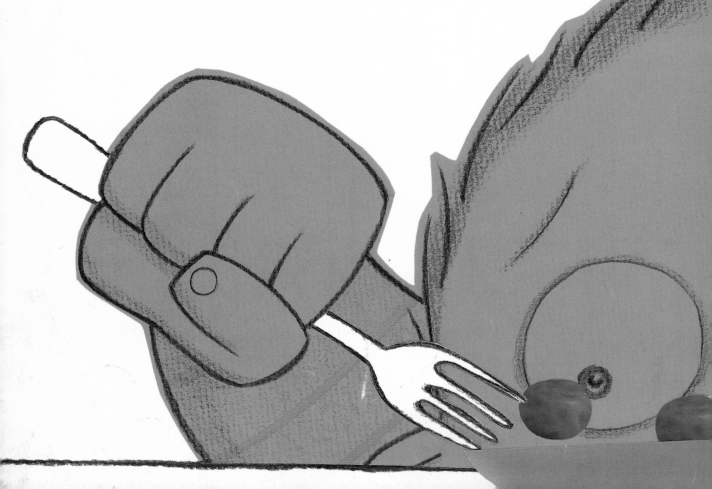

With just the

slightest

touch...

. . . it begins.

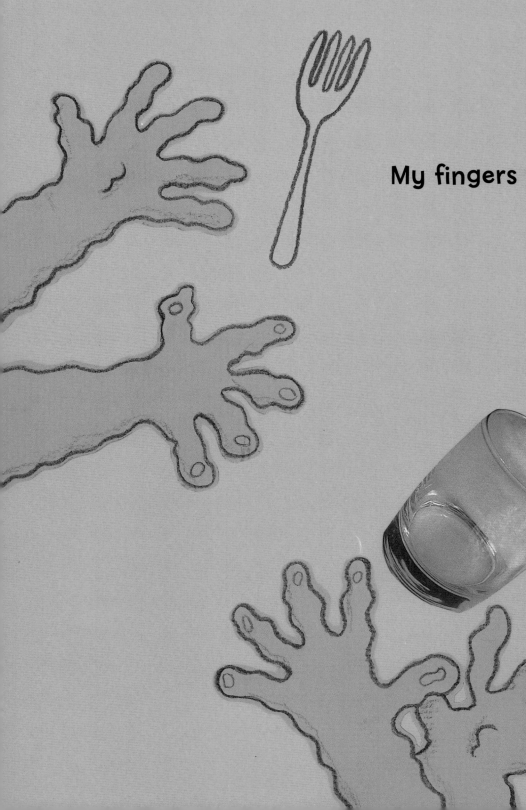

My fingers become all

As the pea rests in my mouth,

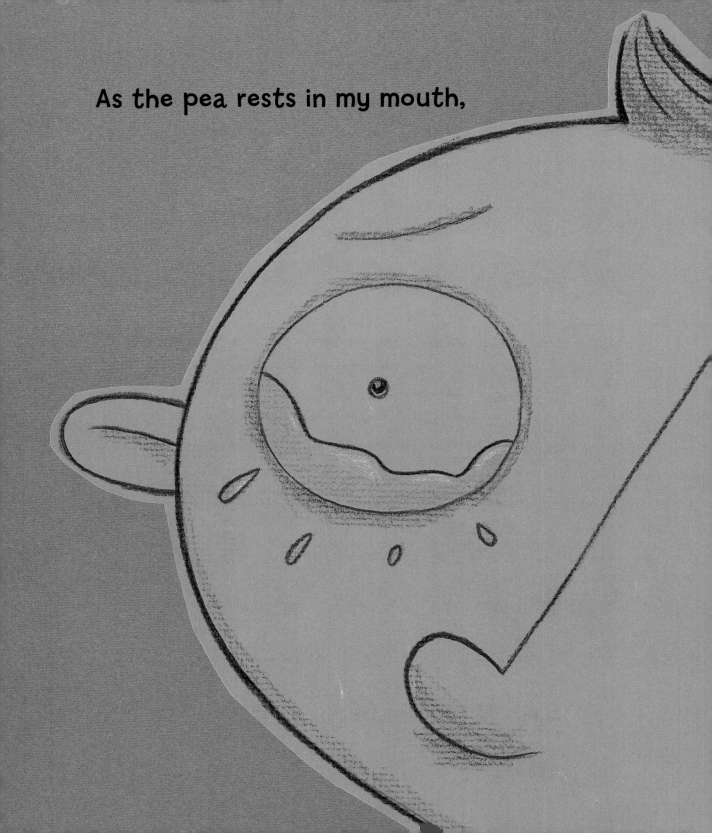

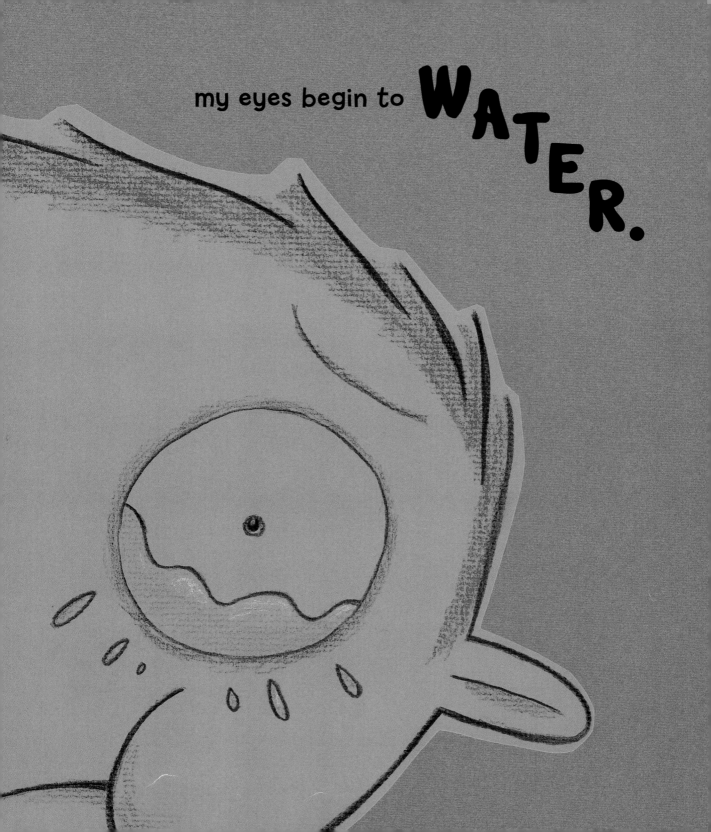

My toes
TWIST and
CURL UP
in my shoes.

I **SQUIRM** in my seat. I try to keep control but the **pea** is too strong. I start to transform into . . .

...a VEGGIE MONSTER!

Ready to **Smash** the chairs!
Ready to *tip* the table!
Ready to...

GREAT pork chops tonight.

. . . GULP!

I swallowed the pea.
I actually swallowed the pea.

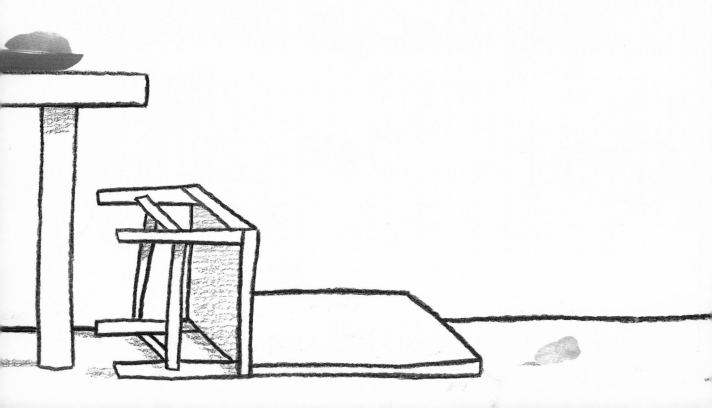

It tasted all right, really.

Well, I guess peas are okay.
But there is still a danger!

Because **tomorrow** is WEDNESDAY,
and on **WEDNESDAY** we have . . .